Weekly Reader Children's Book Club presents

FOX EYES

FOX EYES

by Margaret Wise Brown

Pictures by Garth Williams

PANTHEON BOOKS

Copyright 1951 by Pantheon Books, Inc.
Illustrations Copyright © 1977, by Garth Williams
All rights reserved under International and Pan-American
Copyright Conventions. Published in the United States by
Pantheon Books, a division of Random House, Inc., and
simultaneously in Canada by Random House of Canada Limited,
Toronto. Originally published in 1951 by Pantheon Books.
Manufactured in the United States of America

Library of Congress Cataloging in Publication Data
Brown, Margaret Wise, 1910-1952.   Fox eyes.
SUMMARY: A fox causes consternation among the animals
whose secrets he discovers. Little do they realize that
because of the fox's secret, they have no cause for worry.
1. Foxes—Legends and stories.   [1. Foxes—Fiction.
2. Animals—Fiction]   I. Williams, Garth.   II. Title.
PZ10.3.B7656Fo9   [E]   76-43086
ISBN 0-394-83116-0
ISBN 0-394-93116-5 lib. bdg.

Weekly Reader Children's Book Club Edition

FOX EYES

There was once a spy,
a red fox who came to
spy on the opossums.
There were five of them
and they were supposed to be asleep.

But they weren't.
They each had one eye open.
They were playing possum.
The fox noted all this and
went on his way.

But with their one eye open
the possums had seen
the eye of the fox gleaming
through the hole. They knew
that the fox knew they were
playing possum. And that he
had caught on to their tricks.

A rabbit running through the
field heard the fox nearby
and he froze. He stopped
stark still against the
rabbit-colored grass and
froze to the stillness
of a rock. Even his rabbit
smell was frozen to no
smell, as he crouched there,
invisible as something that
does not move or smell or
look like much.

But the fox peeked through a
hole in a log and watched the
field for a long time. He saw
the rabbit's ears go up.
So he coughed, "Whiskerchew!"
And the rabbit knew the fox had
seen through his tricks and that
it was time to run.

A squirrel was bustling about
under a hazelnut tree.
He frisked his tail
and peered about, then dashed up
a nearby oak tree to a hole
where he hid his nuts.
But the fox was peeking from behind a rock.
And he saw where the little squirrel hid his nuts.
The fox coughed, "Whiskerchew!"

And the little squirrel knew
that the fox had seen his hiding place.

The fox came to the cave where
the bear lived. He peeked through
a hole in the top of the cave,
and he saw a big fat bear sound asleep.
The bear woke up and yawned
till his white teeth gleamed in his
big pink mouth. Then he stretched
and lumbered out of the cave.

The fox followed him. He saw the
bear go to a big stump where he
hid his honey. Then he saw the
bear take a big sticky paw full
of honey out of the old stump.
"Whiskerchew!" the fox coughed.
And at that the bear knew that
someone knew where he hid his honey.
He saw the fox's tail
disappear into the bushes.

Then the fox followed a little fat dog
way out into the middle of a field,
where she went to bury her bone.
"Whiskerchew!" the fox coughed.
And at that the little fat dog knew
that someone knew where she had
buried her bone.

Then the fox climbed an apple tree.
Along the bark of the tree the eye of
a tree toad closed suddenly.
The fox coughed, "Whiskerchew!"
And the tree toad knew that someone
had seen him hiding there in plain
sight against the bark of the tree.

Some children who were
supposed to be taking
a nap in the afternoon
weren't sleeping at all.

"Whiskerchew!" the fox coughed.
And the children knew the fox
knew that they were not sleeping.
All this the fox noted, and he
went on his way.

But that night there was
pandemonium among the animals.
That night the opossums
didn't play possum.

The rabbit ran around all night.

The squirrel got excited and ate
all his nuts.
The little fat dog dug up her bone.

And the bear ate all his honey.
The tree toad stayed in a hole
in the tree.

And the children who were supposed
to be sleeping were not sleepy.

But the fox just yawned.
He sighed and he yawned.
Then he lowered his ears,
curled his big, bushy
tail around him,
closed his eyes,
and went to sleep.
He went to sleep right away
without even thinking about
what he had seen.
For, of course,
the fox could never
remember the next day
what he had seen
the day before.

But no one knows that but the fox.